The Cam Jansen Series

DON'T FORGET ABOUT THE YOUNG CAM JANSEN
SERIES FOR YOUNGER READERS!

Cam Jansen

and the
Green School
Mystery

David A. Adler

illustrated by
Joy Allen

SCHOLASTIC INC.
New York Toronto London Auckland Sydney
Mexico City New Delhi Hong Kong Buenos Aires

ISBN-13: 978-0-545-19907-0
ISBN-10: 0-545-19907-7

Text copyright © 2008 by David A. Adler. Illustrations copyright © 2008
by Penguin Young Readers Group. All rights reserved. Published by
Scholastic Inc., 557 Broadway, New York, NY 10012, by arrangement
with Viking, a division of Penguin Young Readers Group, a member
of Penguin Group (USA) Inc. SCHOLASTIC and associated logos
are trademarks and/or registered trademarks of Scholastic Inc.

12 11 10 9 8 7 6 5 4 3 2   9 10 11 12 13 14/0

Printed in the U.S.A.   40

First Scholastic printing, September 2009

Set in New Baskerville

For Jacob,
my sweet and very smart grandson
—D.A.

To my grandson Curt,
a real helper in keeping my yard green!
—J.A.

Chapter One

"Happy Green Day," Cam Jansen said to her friend Eric Shelton.

Eric smiled and said, "Happy Green Day, Cam."

Cam and Eric were walking to school.

"My sisters are going on the bus," Eric told Cam. "Mom said it's too far for them to walk. But it's not too far for us."

"I plan to do lots more walking," Cam said. "It's good exercise and it doesn't use fossil fuels."

Cam and her classmates had been studying what they could do to help the environment. Today there would be a Green Day assembly at Cam and Eric's school.

Eric showed Cam the bag he was carrying. "I brought in six more empty soda cans," he said.

Cam said, "I have four. I think we brought in more than anyone else."

During the first week of school, Dr. Prell, the school's principal, had visited Cam and Eric's class. She'd asked the children to bring in empty soda cans and bottles.

Dr. Prell had said, "We'll take them to the recycling center. Recycling is good for the environment. And there's a bonus. For each can or bottle we bring in, we'll get a nickel. I hope we bring in lots of cans and bottles and get lots of nickels. If we do, I'll change every two nickels for a dime. Lots of nickels would be too heavy to bring back to school. Your nickels and dimes and the money we made at the book fair will be able to pay for skylights in the front hall. Then, on sunny days, we won't need to turn lights on. That's good for the environment, too."

Children brought in lots of cans and bottles. At first, Mr. Day, the gym teacher, kept the dimes in a large glass bowl. He set the bowl in a locked display case near the gym. When there were too many dimes to fit in the bowl, he put them in paper rolls. He kept the rolls in the display case. Each roll held fifty dimes. It was near the end of the school year. There were lots of dimes in the case.

"We're almost there," Eric said, "and I'm not tired. We should walk to school every day."

At the side of the school, two men were taking bricks and wood off a large truck.

"That must be for the skylights," Eric said. "I'll bet Dr. Prell tells us today that we raised enough money to pay for them."

There were also milk and bread delivery trucks by the side of the school. The milk delivery man was leaving the school. He pushed an empty cart past Cam and Eric. A man walking toward the school was pushing a cart with a big, almost-empty bread box. In it were just a few wrapped loaves of bread.

Cam and Eric walked around to the front of the school. Lots of children had walked. There were buses, too, stopped by the entrance.

"Hey, look at me," Danny Pace called to Cam and Eric. "At least *I* didn't forget what today is."

Danny was wearing a green shirt and green pants. He had even painted his sneakers green.

Cam and Eric waited for Danny at the corner.

"Green Day doesn't mean we should *wear* green," Eric told Danny. "It means we should help keep our *world* green."

"Oh, he knows," Cam said. "He's just trying to be funny."

Danny stood real straight. He smiled and told Cam, "Take a picture of me. I want you to remember how great I look in green. You don't use film, so that's good for the environment."

Cam looked at Danny. She blinked her eyes and said, *"Click!"*

Cam has an amazing memory. People call it a photographic memory because it's as if she has a picture in her head of everything she's seen. When Cam wants to remember something, she just looks at the pictures she has in her head.

Cam says, *"Click!"* when she wants to remember something. She says *"click!"* is the sound her mental camera makes.

Eric said, "I'll also take your picture."

Eric looked at Danny. He blinked his eyes and said, *"Click!"*

"Now close your eyes and turn around," Danny said.

Cam and Eric closed their eyes and turned.

"What's for lunch today?" Danny asked.

"Hey, that's not fair," Eric said. "I looked at you and your clothes. Today's lunch is not on your clothes."

Danny laughed. "It will be," he said. "We're having sloppy Joes. Before I'm done, tomato sauce will be everywhere."

"Well, I know what color your shirt is," Eric said. "It's green."

"How many buttons does it have?"

Eric thought for a moment. Then he shook his head and said, "I don't know."

"I know," Cam said. "There are six buttons down the front of your shirt and one on the pocket. You also have button-down collars, so that's two more. Altogether, your shirt has nine buttons."

"Yeah," Danny said. "Nine."

Cam's real name is Jennifer, but when people found out about her amazing memory, they called her "The Camera." Soon "The Camera" became just "Cam."

"Go on," Eric said. "Ask us something else."

Cam and Eric waited, but Danny didn't ask another question.

"Go on, Danny," Eric said again. "I know what color your pants and your sneakers are. And you're not carrying your book bag."

Cam and Eric waited, but Danny still didn't ask another question.

Cam opened her eyes and turned around.

"Hey," Cam said. "Danny is gone! I'll bet he went into school. It's late. We'd better hurry."

Chapter Two

Cam and Eric hurried into school. Their classroom was near the end of the hall, close to the gym and the cafeteria.

"Look," Eric said as they walked down the hall. "Mr. Day is taking out the dimes."

The display case near the gym was open. Mr. Day was putting the rolls of dimes into a large wooden box.

Eric told Mr. Day, "I brought in six more cans. Cam brought in four."

"Great!" Mr. Day said. "That's fifty cents."

Cam asked, "How much money did we raise?"

"Take a look," Mr. Day said. "Every roll has fifty dimes. That's five dollars."

Lots of rolls were neatly lined up in the box.

"There's enough here to help pay for the skylights," Mr. Day said. "At the assembly, I'll announce how much we raised. Later today, I'll take all the dimes to the bank."

Cam and Eric went to their classroom. The shades were up. The lights were off. Their teacher, Ms. Benson, was using sunlight instead of electric light.

Cam and Eric gave Ms. Benson their soda cans. Then they went to their seats.

Green Hints: What you can do to help the environment was written on the board.

"Copy the Green Hints into your notebooks," Ms. Benson said. "And please use both sides of the paper. Saving paper is saving the environment."

Eric opened his notebook. He started to copy Ms. Benson's Green Hints.

During the day, use sunlight instead of lightbulbs.

Whenever you can, walk don't ride.

Don't waste water.

Whenever you can, use cold water instead of hot water.

Cam didn't copy the hints. She just looked at the board, blinked her eyes, and said, *"Click!*

Green Hints: What you can do to help the environment

1. During the da_ sunlight instead of light bulbs.
2. Whenever ___ walk do_t ride.
3. Don't was__ water___
4. Whenever ___ water instead of hot water.

OUR
PLANE__

"I'm saving paper," she whispered to Eric. "I can remember the hints without writing them."

"I can't," Eric said, and he continued to copy from the board.

Recycle bottles, cans, and newspapers.

Don't waste food. Take only as much as you think you can eat.

Plant a tree.

"Please close your notebooks," Ms. Benson told the class. "It's time to go outside."

The children followed Ms. Benson.

The hall was crowded. Every class in the school was on its way to the assembly.

"Hey," Danny asked, "who knows what's yellow and green?"

Eric looked at Danny's green shirt, pants, and sneakers and answered, "You eating a banana."

"Hey, that's good," Danny said. "But it's wrong."

Ms. Benson turned and faced her class. "Please," she called to the children, "stay in a straight line and walk quietly."

The children followed Ms. Benson. When they reached the front door of the school, Ms. Benson held up her hand and the children stopped.

Outside, next to the flagpole, were a table, a few chairs, and a microphone. Dr. Prell waited there and watched as Mr. Day told the teachers where their classes should stand.

Danny whispered to Eric, "You still didn't tell me what's yellow and green."

"Shh," Eric said.

Mr. Day waved to Ms. Benson, who led her class to the right of the flagpole.

"A moldy chicken," Danny whispered. "That's what's yellow and green."

"That's not even funny," Eric told him. "And we should be quiet."

"Good morning," Dr. Prell said. "This is a great day for our school. It's a *green* day, and we're a *green* school. I am proud to raise this flag."

Dr. Prell pulled a rope and raised a large green flag. Children cheered as it moved up

the flagpole. It stopped just beneath the red, white, and blue American flag.

"We're a green school because we care about the environment."

Children cheered.

"I have an award for the four students who brought in the most soda cans and bottles. They are Ashanti Stevens, Michael Teller, Jennifer Jansen, and Eric Shelton. Please step forward."

Cam, Eric, and the other two children stood by the flagpole. Dr. Prell pinned a large gold-and-green button on each of the children's shirts.

"And now," Dr. Prell said, "Mr. Day will wheel out all those dimes and tell us how much money we raised."

Mr. Day walked into the school.

Dr. Prell smiled. "We raised a lot," she said. "We have enough dimes to help pay for two skylights and a recycling bin."

Children cheered.

"I hope you will continue to bring cans

and bottles for recycling. The money we raise now will be used to buy solar panels."

Mr. Day came back outside, pulling a wagon toward the flagpole. On the wagon was the large wooden box. Mr. Day and another teacher lifted the box onto the table.

"Let's see those dimes," Dr. Prell said.

Mr. Day took the lid off the box and looked in. He seemed surprised.

"Look," he whispered to Dr. Prell.

Dr. Prell looked in the box. Cam and Eric looked in, too. Several bricks were in the box. But the dimes were gone.

Chapter Three

"What happened?" Dr. Prell whispered.

Mr. Day shook his head. He didn't know.

"I put all the rolls of dimes in the box," Mr. Day said. "I put on the lid. Then I came out here to tell the children where to stand."

Dr. Prell looked in the box again. There were still just several bricks in it.

"What do I do now?" Mr. Day asked.

"Please," Dr. Prell whispered, "tell the children how much money they raised."

"But there's nothing in there," Mr. Day whispered. "All the money is gone."

"Don't tell them that! The children were great. They collected lots of bottles and cans. They should know how well they did."

Mr. Day stepped up to the microphone.

"You brought in thousands of bottles and cans. Every day after school, I took them to the recycling center where I got thousands of dimes, which I put into rolls."

Dr. Prell leaned close to Mr. Day and whispered, "They want to know how much money was raised."

"In all, there were one hundred and eighty rolls of dimes."

The children waited.

"That's nine hundred dollars."

The children and teachers cheered.

Cam whispered to Eric, "That's how much was stolen."

"But you'll find all those dimes," Eric whispered. "They were here this morning. What happened to them is a mystery, and you'll solve it."

"I'm not so sure," Cam said, and shook her head.

Dr. Prell thanked Mr. Day. Then she thanked all the children.

"Congratulations. You did a great job. Keep bringing in bottles and cans. There's lots more we can do to help our environment. Now please wait for Mr. Day to call your class. Then return to your rooms."

The four children who had won gold-and-green buttons were told not to talk about the missing dimes. Two of the winners, Ashanti

Stevens and Michael Teller, returned to their teachers. Cam and Eric didn't. They stepped back and stood by the flagpole. They watched as Mr. Day called one class after another.

When the classes had all entered the building, Mr. Day turned to Dr. Prell. "I think I can solve this mystery," he said. "After all, those dimes were really heavy. No one could have carried them out of the school. They must be hidden somewhere."

Eric said, "We're good at finding things."

Dr. Prell turned and noticed Cam and Eric.

"Why aren't you with your class?" she asked.

Eric pointed to Cam and said, "Cam has solved lots of mysteries. I'll bet she can find the missing dimes."

"We just want to help," Cam said.

"They're good kids," Mr. Day said. "And Cam has a great memory. She saw me this morning when I was emptying the display case. Maybe she remembers something."

"Well," Dr. Prell said, "do you remember anything?"

Cam closed her eyes. She said, *"Click!*

"This morning," Cam said, with her eyes still closed, "we saw Mr. Day put rolls of dimes into the wooden box."

"Lots of rolls," Eric said.

"They were very heavy," Cam said.

"That's right," Mr. Day said. "No one could have just carried all of them out of the building. I think they're still here, but there are lots of places to look. Cam and Eric can help us."

Dr. Prell said, "I don't like children to miss their lessons."

"Please," Mr. Day said.

Dr. Prell looked at Cam and Eric. "Okay," she told Mr. Day. "They can help you look. But only until lunchtime. If you don't find the dimes by then, they have to go back to class."

"Yeah!" Eric said. "And you'll see. We'll solve this mystery."

"I'm going to speak with the custodian, Mrs. Adams," Dr. Prell said. "She's very observant. Maybe she noticed something."

Dr. Prell walked toward the school entrance.

"I hope we can find those dimes," Cam whispered to Eric. "But right now I don't remember any clues."

"Well," Mr. Day said to Cam, "let's start looking."

"But where?" Cam asked, and shook her head. "I think whoever took the money was smart. He put bricks in the box so it would be heavy. He didn't want you to know the money was missing until you opened the box. And smart people find great hiding places."

"I think I know where to look," Mr. Day said. "Let's look in the gym."

Chapter Four

Cam and Eric followed Mr. Day into the building.

"The gym is real close to the display case," Mr. Day said. "And that's where I left the box of dimes."

"I don't think it's here," Eric said when they entered the gym. "This is just a big empty room. There's no place to hide anything."

"Come with me," Mr. Day said.

He took them to the locker room.

Mr. Day said, "I think they're in one of the lockers."

Eric began to quickly open one locker

after another. The metal doors clanged and squeaked as they swung open.

Cam held her hands to her ears.

Eric was done opening the front row of lockers.

"There's nothing in any of these," Eric said.

"I didn't mean those lockers," Mr. Day said. "I meant these."

By his desk were three lockers with pad-locks.

"But I can't open those," Eric said. "They're locked."

"This first one is mine," Mr. Day said. "I keep my papers and lunch in here. But these two are mysteries to me. Locks have been on them since I came here."

"The dimes can't be in those," Eric said, pointing to the two other lockers. "The dimes were just stolen, and you said those have been locked for years."

Mr. Day pointed to his head and said, "You're not thinking like a criminal." He smiled. "Let's say this lock belongs to someone in this building. He has a key to it. He stole the dimes, unlocked the locker, put the coins in, and locked it again. Then, every day, he'll sneak back in here and take out a few rolls of dimes."

"That's some plan," Cam said.

"Oh, sure," Mr. Day said. "Those coins were on display for a long time. Every few days, I put in more rolls of dimes. The thief probably passed by the case all the time. He doesn't have a key to the display case, so he was just waiting for me to unlock it and take the money out."

Eric said, "We just have to hide here and watch those two lockers. When someone takes out the money, we'll be here to catch him."

Mr. Day shook his head and said, "No."

"We could get a video camera," Eric said. "It could tape everyone who comes in here."

"No," Mr. Day said again, and shook his head. "I'll just open the lockers."

Mr. Day took a large ring of keys from his desk drawer.

Cam asked, "How many keys do you have?"

"A lot, maybe one hundred," Mr. Day said. "Whenever I find a key in the gym or outside, I save it. Someone might come looking for it. I put it on this ring. With all these keys, I'm sure I can open those locks."

Mr. Day tried to push a key into one of the padlocks. It didn't fit. He tried another key. That one also didn't fit. Cam and Eric sat on a bench and watched Mr. Day try one key after another. But none of the keys fit.

"Don't worry," Eric said, "Cam will *click* and remember something that will help us find the money."

"Not yet. Don't do any of that *clicking* stuff," Mr. Day said. "I want to solve this mystery. I just have to borrow something from Mrs. Adams."

Mr. Day left the locker room.

Eric said, "I don't think the money is in the lockers."

"I agree," Cam said. "And I don't think the money is still in the school. A thief would not want to come back here after everyone knows the money was stolen."

Eric laughed. "What would anyone do with all those dimes?"

"He'll change them at a bank."

Mr. Day walked back into the locker room. He was holding a pair of clippers with long handles. Dr. Prell was with him.

"Now we'll find those dimes," he said.

"Maybe," Dr. Prell said. "Or maybe we'll find what someone left here a long time ago."

Chapter Five

"Whose locks are these?" Dr. Prell asked.

"The first one, the one near my desk, is mine," Mr. Day answered. "The other two locks were here when I came to this school. I don't know whose they are."

Dr. Prell said, "Break them open."

Mr. Day held the clippers by the ends of the long handles. The blades were set to cut the lock.

Snap!

The lock was cut open.

Dr. Prell took off the broken lock. She opened the locker and took out an open box of crackers. She shook a few crackers onto Mr. Day's desk.

"Yuck!" Mr. Day said. "They're moldy."

"That's all that was in there, a box of moldy crackers," Dr. Prell said. "Break open the other locker."

Mr. Day cut the second lock. There were just papers in that locker.

"I'll open the third locker," Mr. Day said.

He was about to snip the lock.

"Wait!" Eric told him. "Don't you have a key to your own lock?"

"Yes, I do."

He opened the lock. Dr. Prell looked in the locker. "There are lots of papers in here," she said. "It's a mess."

"But there are no dimes," Mr. Day told her. "We still don't know where the money is. I was wrong. The thief did not hide the money here. I'll take these clippers back to Mrs. Adams."

Dr. Prell took a cell phone from her pocket and said, "I'll call the police." She pressed a few buttons on her cell phone and held it close to her ear. "Hello. I'm reporting a robbery." Dr. Prell told the police officer about the stolen dimes.

Mr. Day returned to the locker room.

"The police will be here soon," Dr. Prell told him.

"Jennifer and Eric," she said, "please go to your class. And don't talk about the missing dimes. Everyone worked so hard

to raise all that money. They don't have to
know it was stolen. If we don't find it, I'll
find another way to pay for the skylights."

"Don't worry," Eric told her. "I'm sure
Cam can *click* and find a clue and solve the
mystery."

Cam closed her eyes. She said, *"Click!"*

"Please," Dr. Prell said, "you don't need
to *click*. Now it's up to the police."

"I'm looking at the wooden box and all
the dimes," Cam said with her eyes closed.
"There were lots of dimes."

"I don't need a photographic memory to
know that," Mr. Day said.

Cam said, *"Click!"* again. Then she said, "The thief left the wood box."

"I know that, too," Mr. Day said.

"Please," Dr. Prell told Cam and Eric, "go to your class."

"Let's go," Eric told Cam.

Cam's eyes were still closed.

Eric took Cam's hand and walked with her out of the gym.

As they walked, Cam said, *"Click!"* She said it again and again.

"Do you see anything?" Eric asked. "Did you find a clue?"

"No," Cam said, and shook her head. "I still don't know how someone took all those dimes out of here. If I solve that mystery, I'll find the thief."

Cam's eyes were still closed. Eric led her into their classroom.

"Where were you?" Ms. Benson asked.

Eric whispered to her. He told her about the missing money.

"That's terrible," she said.

"We didn't find the dimes," Eric whispered, "so Dr. Prell called the police."

"I hope they find the money," Ms. Benson whispered back. "Now Jennifer, please open your eyes."

Cam opened her eyes.

The classroom lights were off. The shades were up. Sun was shining through the windows.

Cam and Eric went to their seats.

Ms. Benson went on with the lesson.

"Why should we plant trees?"

A few of Cam's classmates raised their hands.

"Look!" Beth called out before anyone could answer Ms. Benson's question. "The police are here."

Beth pointed outside. A police car had stopped by the front of the school.

Danny held out his hands and said, "Oh, please don't arrest me! I'm innocent."

Chapter Six

"I arrest Danny in the name of the law," Beth said. "I arrest you for telling bad jokes."

"Me?!" Danny said. He pretended to be surprised. "I tell great jokes. Like what did the big sunflower say to the little sunflower?"

"Flowers don't talk," Beth said. "And if they did, and they weren't talking to me, I wouldn't listen. That's just being nosy!"

"Look," Amy said, and pointed outside. "Two police officers got out of the car. They're coming into school."

Beth said, "I'll bet Cam knows why they're here."

"Let's get back to our lesson," Ms. Benson said. "Jennifer, can you tell the class why it's good to plant trees?"

"Trees are good for recycling," Cam answered. "They take in carbon dioxide and recycle it as oxygen. We need oxygen to breathe."

Eric raised his hand.

"The roots are good for the ground," he said. "Roots hold on to dirt and keep it from washing away in the rain."

Danny called out, "Eric knows about dirt, but he doesn't know what the big sunflower said to the little one. It said, 'Hi there, bud!'"

Beth said, "That's not even funny."

"Why should we try to burn less fossil fuel?" Ms. Benson asked.

Beth raised her hand. "Coal and oil are fossil fuels," she answered. "We only have a certain amount of them. If we use too much, we might use them all up. And when they burn, they put bad gasses in the air."

Cam slid down in her seat so Ms. Benson wouldn't see her. Then she closed her eyes and whispered, *"Click!"*

"Did you remember something?" Eric whispered. "Did you remember a clue?"

Cam shook her head. She whispered, "Not yet, but I'm sure I'm missing something. I just don't know what."

"What about solar and wind power?" Ms. Benson asked.

Hector raised his hand.

"Every day that the sun shines we have more solar energy," Hector answered. "Every time the wind blows we have wind power. They don't get used up and they don't burn."

"Very good," Ms. Benson said. "Now, I have a special project for each of us. I want us all not only to go to a green school, I want us to live in green homes. I want each of you to make at least three changes in your homes, three things to help save our environment. By next Friday I want a detailed report on the changes you made."

"Hey," Danny said, "I'm hungry."

"I'll put a fluorescent bulb in my lamp," Eric said. "That will save energy."

"I'm running out of energy," Danny said. "I need people fuel. I need to eat."

Cam whispered, "I forgot all about lunch. The school lunch is sloppy Joes. That's chopped meat and sauce on hero rolls. Lots of hero rolls."

"So what?"

Cam closed her eyes and said, *"Click!"*

"Did you remember something?" Eric asked.

"Click!" Cam said again.

"Please," Ms. Benson told the class, "line up for lunch."

"Let's go," Eric said to Cam.

Her eyes were still closed. Cam had brought her lunch from home. Eric took it from Cam's cubby. With his other hand he led Cam to the back of the line.

"Follow me," Ms. Benson told the class.

The children walked quietly in a double line out of the room. Cam and Eric were at the very back of the line. Cam opened her eyes just as they were walking past the main office.

Cam told Eric, "I remembered something that might solve the mystery."

"What mystery?" Beth asked. "Is something wrong? Was something broken or stolen? Is that why the police are here?"

Eric said, "We're not supposed to talk about it."

"About what?" Danny asked.

"If I told you that," Eric said, "I would be talking about it."

Ms. Benson stopped the class. They were by the entrance to the cafeteria.

"Let's go," Cam said. "I have to talk with Mrs. Apple, the cafeteria lady. I have to ask her something."

"What?" Eric asked. "What do you have to ask Mrs. Apple?"

"Tell me, too," Danny said.

Cam said, "I have to ask her if she can make me a sandwich. If she can't make a sandwich, I might have solved the mystery."

"Tell me!" Danny shouted. "What mystery?"

Cam didn't answer. She left the line and hurried past the other children in her class and Ms. Benson. She was about to go into the cafeteria when Ms. Benson called to her.

Chapter Seven

"Jennifer, come back here," Ms. Benson said. "We'll all go in together."

Cam stopped. She turned and told Ms. Benson, "But I'm not going in for lunch. I have to ask Mrs. Apple a question. It's about—" Cam paused, then said quietly, "You know what it's about."

"Oh, yes. Go ahead."

"I want to go, too," Eric said.

"Go ahead," Ms. Benson told Eric.

"Hey, what about me?" Danny asked. "I'm the one who is really hungry."

"Get back on line," Ms. Benson told Danny. "You'll go in with everyone else."

"Sure," Danny complained, "by the time I get to eat, my sloppy Joe won't even be sloppy anymore. Joe's shirt will be tucked in and his hair will be combed. He'll be neat Joe!"

Cam and Eric hurried past the children waiting on line to get their lunches. They walked into the kitchen.

"Mrs. Apple, can I get a cheese sandwich?" Cam asked an old woman.

Mrs. Apple wore a white apron and white gloves. Her hair was in a net. She held a bread knife and was cutting a hero roll in half.

Mrs. Apple said, "Today's lunch is sloppy Joes. I can't stop and make you a special sandwich."

"You can't because you're busy," Cam asked, "or you can't because all you·have are hero rolls?"

Mrs. Apple put down the roll she had just cut.

"Well," she said, "I can't for both reasons. This morning the baker brought me hero rolls. He didn't bring me regular sandwich bread."

"That's just what I thought," Cam said. "Let's go," she told Eric. "We have to speak to Dr. Prell."

Cam quickly left the kitchen. Eric followed her.

"I don't get it," Eric said. "You brought your lunch from home. Why do you want a cheese sandwich?"

Cam and Eric hurried to Ms. Benson.

"We need to see Dr. Prell," Cam told her teacher. Then Cam leaned close and whispered, "You know what it's about."

"Go ahead," Ms. Benson said.

"She's probably in her office," Cam said. "She's probably there telling the police all about the stolen dimes."

They hurried to the main office.

"We need to see Dr. Prell," Cam told Mrs. Wayne, the principal's secretary.

"Why?" Mrs. Wayne asked. "Was there a fight? Is someone hurt? Is someone sick?"

"No," Cam told her. "It's about the dimes."

"Oh," Mrs. Wayne said. She looked to be sure no one else was listening. Then she leaned forward and whispered, "Do you know all those dimes were stolen? Right now

Dr. Prell is telling two nice police officers what happened."

"Are they in her office?" Cam asked.

Mrs. Wayne shook her head and said, "They're not here. They went to the gym to see Mr. Day."

"Let's go," Cam said.

"Why?" Eric asked. "What's going on?"

"I remembered something I saw when we came to school this morning," Cam told him. "I think I might know who stole the dimes."

"What did you remember?"

"Let's go to the gym," Cam said. "I'll tell you everything on the way."

"And please," Eric said as he followed Cam. "Tell me why you wanted a sandwich?"

Cam laughed.

"I don't want another cheese sandwich. My dad already made me one. I just wanted to know if Mrs. Apple had sandwich bread."

"Why?" Eric asked. "Hero rolls are better."

Cam said, "When we came to school this morning, the man delivering the milk pushed an empty cart past us. He had brought in all the milk and was going back to his truck."

"You think he stole the money?"

"No," Cam said. "Do you remember what the man from the bakery had on his cart?"

Eric shook his head. He didn't remember.

"There were only a few loaves of bread on his cart."

Cam and Eric walked past the empty display case just outside the gym.

"Why didn't he bring in the loaves of bread with the hero rolls?" Cam asked. "And if he delivered bread, why couldn't Mrs. Apple make me a sandwich?"

"Maybe she was busy," Eric said. "Maybe she didn't have cheese."

"No," Cam said as they entered the gym. "She said she didn't have sandwich bread."

Two police officers were in the gym, a tall woman and a not-so-tall man with a short beard. They were talking with Dr. Prell and Mr. Day.

"Hey," the not-so-tall police officer said when he saw Cam. "There's the girl with the

photographic memory. Do you remember
me?" he asked Cam. "I'm Officer Oppen."

"And I'm Officer Davis," the other police
officer said.

Cam nodded. She remembered them.

"Tell me," Officer Oppen said. "Is there
some picture in your head that will help us
find the stolen money?"

"I think so," Cam said. "I think I might
know who took the dimes and how he got
them out of the school."

Chapter Eight

Officer Oppen opened his detective pad.

"Please, tell us," Officer Davis said. "Who took the dimes?"

"This morning," Cam said, "we saw someone from the bakery push a cart into school. On it were what looked like just a few wrapped loaves of bread."

Officer Davis shook her head. "Of course the man from the bakery had bread on the cart."

Officer Oppen closed his detective pad.

Cam said, "But we have sloppy Joes for lunch. He must have already brought in a cart loaded with hero rolls. Why didn't he bring the bread in with the heroes?"

"Tell them the rest," Eric said. "Tell them what happened when you asked Mrs. Apple for a sandwich."

"She didn't have sandwich bread," Cam said. "That's because the man from the bakery wasn't bringing in loaves of bread. He was bringing in bricks! He took the bricks from the ones on the side of the school. Then he put the bricks in bread wrappers so no one would know what he was doing."

Dr. Prell said, "The bricks were for the skylights."

"The bricks he snuck into school were the ones I found in the box," Mr. Day said. "He used them to replace the dimes. That way, when I lifted the box it felt like there were rolls of dimes in it."

"But there weren't," Eric said. "The dimes were gone."

Officer Davis asked Dr. Prell, "What bakery do you use?"

Dr. Prell thought for a moment. Then she shook her head. She didn't know.

"I know," Cam said.

Cam closed her eyes. She said, "*Click!*

"This morning I saw the truck," Cam said with her eyes closed. "The name of the bakery is Angela's Wings. It was truck number seven. The telephone number was also on the side of the truck."

Cam told them the bakery's telephone number.

Officer Oppen called the bakery. He asked about truck number seven. Then he said, "Please send it back to the school on Jefferson Street."

When he was done talking on the cell phone, Officer Oppen told Dr. Prell and the others, "Truck seven hasn't come back. The driver is still making deliveries."

"Or maybe he's at the bank," Mr. Day said. "Maybe he's changing lots of rolls of dimes for dollar bills."

"The man I spoke with will call him," Officer Oppen said. "I didn't say anything about the money. He probably thinks you need more bread."

"We'll wait for him," Officer Davis said.

"Jennifer and Eric," Dr. Prell said, "you can go back to the cafeteria. We'll tell you if you were right about the missing dimes."

Cam and Eric returned to the cafeteria. Cam sat at a table with Amy, Beth, Hector, and Danny. Eric went to the counter to get the school lunch.

"Look at me," Danny said. "I have a green shirt and a red mustache and beard."

Danny had spread tomato sauce on his face. Sauce had also spilled on his shirt and pants.

Beth told Cam, "Mrs. Apple gave him a sloppy Joe, and now we have a sloppy Danny."

"Hey, I'd like that," Danny said. "I'd like a sandwich named after me."

"I wouldn't eat it," Amy told him. "It would probably taste funny."

Cam opened her lunch bag. She took out a cheese sandwich.

Eric came to the table with a tray and a sloppy Joe.

"Can you tell us why you're late to lunch?" Amy asked. "Can you tell us what's going on?"

Cam's mouth was full of bread and cheese. Eric's mouth was filled with meat and sauce. They both shook their heads. They couldn't tell Amy about the mystery.

"Five minutes," Mrs. Apple called out. "You have five minutes to finish your lunches and clear your tables."

"Oh, my," Eric said. He quickly took another bite of his sloppy Joe. "Gye valve noo barry."

"What did he say?" Danny asked.

Cam told him, "Eric said, 'I have to hurry.'"

Cam, Eric, and the others finished their lunches. They cleared the table. They were on their way back to their classroom when Mr. Day stopped them.

"Dr. Prell wants to see you in her office," he said.

"Me?" Danny asked. "What did I do?"

"No, not you. She wants to see Cam and Eric."

Cam and Eric followed Mr. Day to the principal's office. Dr. Prell, the two police officers, and a young man were there. Next to Dr. Prell's desk was a cart. On it was a bakery box loaded with rolls of coins.

"I tell you," the young man said, "I don't know how those coins got in my truck."

"I think I know," Officer Oppen said.

"You'll have to come with us," Officer Davis told him.

"Thank you," Officer Oppen said to Cam and Eric as he walked out with the delivery man. "You helped us solve this mystery."

"Yes, thank you," Dr. Prell said.

"Maybe you should give them a reward," Mr. Day said.

"We already got a reward," Eric said. "We got gold-and-green buttons."

"And finding the dimes will help our environment. That's also our reward," Cam said.

Eric agreed.

"Before you go back to class," Mr. Day said, "I just thought of something really funny. The dimes are in rolls."

No one laughed.

"Don't you get it?" Mr. Day asked. "The thief delivered hero rolls and he stole dime rolls."

"I got it," Dr. Prell said. "It's just not funny."

Eric said, "But we know who would think that's funny. Don't we, Cam?"

Cam and Eric laughed. "Danny," they said together.

Dr. Prell said, "He told me the silliest joke this morning. It was about a talking sunflower."

"We heard it," Eric told her.

"Let's go back to class," Cam said, "but not to hear more jokes. This afternoon Ms. Benson is teaching us geometry, something about triangles. I don't want to miss it."

Cam and Eric went back to class.

Just a few days later, the skylights were in. The front hall of Cam and Eric's school was lit with sunlight.

A Cam Jansen Memory Game

Take another look at the picture opposite page 1. Study it. Blink your eyes and say, *"Click!"* Then turn back here and answer the questions at the bottom of the page. Please, first study the picture, *then* look at the questions.

1. Is the sun shining?

2. Is Cam wearing a hat?

3. Is there a school bus in the picture?

4. Are Cam and Eric wearing backpacks?

5. Is Eric holding a bag in his left hand or his right hand?

6. Are Cam and Eric the only ones walking to school?